Nate the Great
and The
Snowy Trail

Nate the Great
and The
Snowy Trail

by Marjorie Weinman Sharmat

illustrated by Marc Simont

A Yearling Book

Published by
Yearling
an imprint of
Random House Children's Books
a division of Random House, Inc.
New York

Visit us on the Web! www.randomhouse.com/kids

Educators and librarians, for a variety of teaching tools, visit us at www.randomhouse.com/teachers

ISBN: 0-440-46276-2
Reprinted by arrangement with the Putnam Publishing Group, Inc.
Printed in the United States of America
One Previous Edition
September 2005
70 69 68 67 66 65 64 63 62 61 60
UPR

I, Nate the Great,

am a detective.

This morning I was a cold detective.

I was standing in the snow

with my dog, Sludge,

building a snow dog

and a snow detective.

They looked like Sludge and me.

They were cold and white and wet.

And so were we.

Rosamond came along.

Rosamond is strange most of the time.

Today was one of those times.

She was pulling her four cats,

Super Hex, Big Hex, Little Hex,

and Plain Hex, on a sled.

She went up to the snow detective.

"I lost your birthday present,"

she said to him.

The snow detective did not answer.

I did.

"That detective is one hour old.

Why are you giving him

a birthday present?"

Rosamond looked at me.

"Oh, it's for *you*," she said.

"My birthday is July 12," I said.

"This is the middle of winter."

"I believe in giving early,"

Rosamond said.

She pointed to her sled.

"I was pulling your present
and my cats
on my sled,
but the present fell off
along the way."

"Do you know when and where

it happened?" I asked.

"Yes," Rosamond said.

"I was feeling drippy.

Snow from the trees

was falling on me.

Then all of a sudden

the sled felt lighter.

I turned around

and looked at it.

Your present was gone.

I walked around and around

in the snow,

but I couldn't find it.

It has a Happy Birthday card on it.

Will you look for your present?"

I, Nate the Great,

knew that Rosamond's present

must be strange.

But I am a detective.

And the present was lost.

"I, Nate the Great,

will take your case,"
I said.
"Tell me what the present is,
so I will know
what to look for."

"Oh, I can't tell you *that*,"
Rosamond said.
"It would spoil the surprise.
But it could be
big or small
or medium size
or square or pointy
or flat or bulgy.
Or red or blue
or green or black
or plaid or polka-dotted or . . ."
Suddenly I, Nate the Great,
knew something.
I did not want this case.
"How can I find something
if I do not know

what I am looking for?" I asked.

"You're a great detective,

aren't you?" Rosamond said.

She walked away

and pulled her cats behind her.

Sludge and I went inside.

I left a note for my mother.

Dear mother,
I am going out
into the cold world
to look for something strange.
I will be back.
Love,
Nate The Great

I put on a dry pair of mittens.

Then Sludge and I

went out into the snow.

Rosamond had given me a clue,

but she did not know it.

She had told me

that the sled felt lighter

the moment the present was not on it.

I, Nate the Great, knew

that the present must be heavy.

But it had to fit on the sled

with the four cats.

So I knew it was not as big

as a dead tree

or a broken sofa

or an old door

or some other strange thing

that only Rosamond could think of.

I, Nate the Great,
was glad about that.
I looked down at the snow.
I saw Rosamond's footprints.
I saw sled marks.
Some came toward my house.
Some went away from my house.

Hmm. I, Nate the Great,
had an idea.
If I followed the prints
that led toward my house,
I could see the path
that Rosamond took to my house.

Perhaps the present
was lying in the snow
along the path.
Sludge and I
walked forward in the snow
while we watched Rosamond's
footprints
going backward in the snow.
It was a long, cold walk.
The snow crunched.
Icicles hung from the trees.
All at once,
under a tree,
Rosamond's footprints
went in a wide circle.
Around and around.

This must be
where she lost my present
and was looking for it!
Sludge sniffed the snow.

I looked in the snow

for a package

or the snow print

of a package.

But the snow

next to the sled marks

was unbroken.

I, Nate the Great, was puzzled.

How could something

drop off the sled

and not be in the snow

or leave a mark

in the snow?

There were no footprints either.

So I, Nate the Great, knew

that no one had come along

and taken the birthday present.

But how did the present

get off the sled,

and where was it?

"This is a tough, ice-cold case,"

I said to Sludge.

Sludge shivered.

We trudged on.

We saw Annie and her dog, Fang.

Sludge shivered some more.

He was afraid of Fang.

I, Nate the Great,

was afraid of Fang.

Fang ran toward us.

Sludge leaped over

a big pile of snow.

I had never seen Sludge

leap that high.

"Fang is so friendly,"

Annie said.

She was making a snow dog.

It looked just like Fang.

It had icicles for teeth.

They were long and sharp and pointed.

Just like Fang's teeth.

But I liked them better.

They would melt.

I said, "I am looking

for a heavy birthday present

that could be

big or small

or medium size

or square or pointy

or flat or bulgy.

Or red or blue

or green or black

or plaid or polka-dotted

or any number of things.

But there is one thing for sure.

It is strange."

"Rosamond was here," Annie said.

"But she left.

I have not seen anything strange

since then."

"What did she do and say?"

I asked.

"Well," Annie said, "I was inside

drinking hot chocolate.

Rosamond came in.

She told me she had

a birthday present for you.

She said it was outside

on her sled

with her four cats.

She wouldn't tell me

what it was.

But she said it was

the most beautiful present ever."

"That is a good clue," I said.

"Rosamond thinks scorpions and spiders

and bats are beautiful.

So I, Nate the Great,

now know I am looking

for something ugly."

I thanked Annie for her help.

I called to Sludge.

He was hiding behind

a pile of snow.

We started out again.

"We are looking for something

strange, heavy, and ugly,"

I said.

I saw a snow castle up ahead.

Claude was sitting inside it.

Claude was always losing things.

"Look what I found," Claude said.

"A snow castle."

"Your luck is changing," I said.

"Perhaps you have found

a strange, heavy, and ugly

birthday present?"

"Who would want to find *that*?"

Claude asked.

It was a good question.

But I, Nate the Great,

did not want to answer it.

"I saw an ugly birthday card

at a store this morning,"

Claude said. "Rosamond was buying it."

"Aha!" I said.

"What else did Rosamond buy?"

"She bought six cartons

of milk," Claude said.

I, Nate the Great,

was sorry to hear that.

"Six cartons of milk?" I said.

I, Nate the Great, did not want

a birthday present

that was cold and white and wet.

I was already colder

and whiter

and wetter

than I had ever been.

I said good-bye to Claude.

"Enjoy your castle," I said.

"Don't lose it."

"How can I lose a castle?"

Claude asked.

"Only you know how," I said.

Sludge and I went to Rosamond's house.

I said, "I do not know

where my birthday present is,

but I know *what* it is.

Please open your refrigerator."

Rosamond opened her refrigerator.

I saw tuna fish, cat food,

and a melting snow cat inside.

"Aha!" I said. "No milk!

You bought six cartons of milk

this morning, but now you have none.

You put them on your sled

to take to me.

And that was the birthday present

you lost on the way to my house."

Rosamond took out the snow cat

and licked it.

"Why would I buy you
a strange present
like six cartons of milk?"
she asked.

29

I, Nate the Great,

knew better

than to tell Rosamond why.

"The milk was for my cats,"

Rosamond said. "They drank it up."

I, Nate the Great,

was getting nowhere.

This case was more ice-cold than ever.

I tried to think warm thoughts.

I thought about my warm house.

I thought about warm pancakes.

I said good-bye to Rosamond.

Sludge and I trudged home

through the snow.

Sludge was still shivering.

At home I ate some warm pancakes.

I gave Sludge a warm bone.
Sludge is a great detective.
But all he had done
was shiver and leap
in the snow.
Leap in the snow.
Leap. Hmm.
I, Nate the Great,
thought about that.

Did Sludge know something

I didn't know?

I thought about footprints

and sled marks

in the snow

and snow that had no marks in it,

and six cartons of milk
and other chilly things.
The milk
was for Rosamond's four cats.
But she bought *six* cartons.
Who or what needed
the two extra cartons of milk?
And what would Rosamond think
was the most beautiful
present ever?

Suddenly I, Nate the Great,

knew what my present was,

and where it was,

and how it got there.

I said to Sludge,

"I know what is heavy, strange, and ugly

and can get off a sled

without landing in the snow.

The case is solved,

and you were a big help.

But we must go out

into the cold world again."

Sludge and I went back

to the place

where Rosamond had lost the present.

This time I did not look down
at the snow.
I looked up
at the tree.
There was my birthday present
sitting high up in the tree!

It was heavy and strange
and ugly, all right.
It was the biggest cat
I had ever seen.
It was bigger than Super Hex.
It was almost as big as Sludge.
It was almost as big as me,
Nate the Great.
It was a monster.
It had a Happy Birthday card
hanging from a ribbon
around its neck.
Now I knew why Rosamond
had bought six cartons of milk
when she had only four cats.
This monster cat

she was giving me

was so big

it needed two cartons of milk.

And I knew why

I had not seen the birthday present

or marks from the birthday present

in the snow

next to the sled.

The birthday present

had not touched the snow.

It had *leaped*

from the sled

into the tree.

Now I knew everything

except what I was going to do

with my birthday present.

Sludge and I went back
to Rosamond's house.

"The case is solved," I said.

"I found my birthday present
up a tree."

"Oh, good!" Rosamond said.

"His name is Super Duper Hex.

I got him from the same place

I got Super Hex, Big Hex,

Little Hex, and Plain Hex.

I wanted to keep him.

But he fights with my cats and wins.

He scratches, claws, and bites.

But nobody's perfect.

Happy birthday!"

Sometimes, being a great detective
is not great.

Sludge and I trudged home
through the snow.

We passed the tree
where my birthday present
was still sitting.

He liked it there.

Maybe he would sit there
forever.

Or maybe he would jump down
and follow us home.

Sludge and I kept walking.

I, Nate the Great,

knew two new things.

Never look up.

And never look back.

Sludge and I went home

and sat by the fire.

I was glad I had

only one birthday a year.

～ Extra ～
Fun Activities!

What's Inside

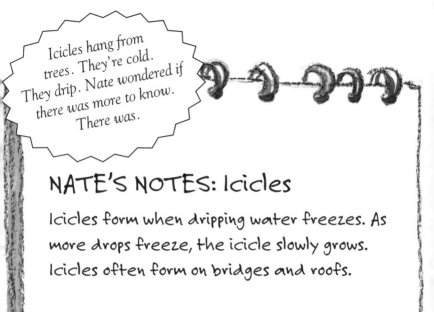

Icicles hang from trees. They're cold. They drip. Nate wondered if there was more to know. There was.

NATE'S NOTES: Icicles

Icicles form when dripping water freezes. As more drops freeze, the icicle slowly grows. Icicles often form on bridges and roofs.

Are there icicles outside right now? Then try this. Draw a picture of an icicle. Now go outside and look closely at one. Notice the shape. What is the surface like? Smooth or bumpy? Do icicles look the way you thought?

About a hundred years ago, a hundred-foot-long icicle formed on an overpass in Edinburgh, Scotland. It may have been the biggest icicle ever! Proud residents had a postcard made of the giant.

NATE'S NOTES:

The Trails Cats Leave

Super Duper Hex didn't leave a trail. Leaping cats don't. But Nate wondered if he'd ever need to track a cat. He decided to study up. Here's what he learned.

TRACKING WORDS:

PRINT: the impression made by one foot

TRAIL: a series of prints

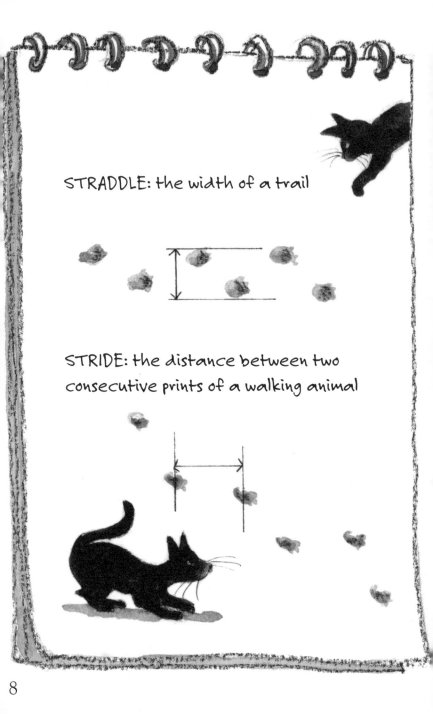

STRADDLE: the width of a trail

STRIDE: the distance between two consecutive prints of a walking animal

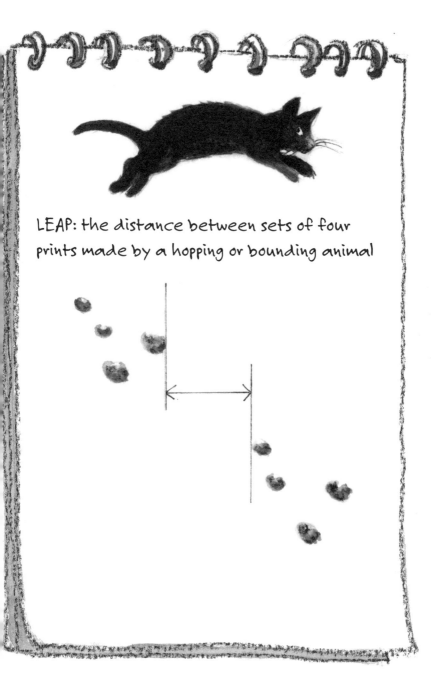

LEAP: the distance between sets of four prints made by a hopping or bounding animal

House Cat Tracks

WHERE YOU FIND THEM: near homes and towns

STRADDLE: 2 inches
STRIDE: 4½ to 5 inches

FRONT PRINT: I inch long, I inch wide

HIND PRINT: slightly smaller

The size of cats' paws varies— just like human feet!

Cats are "perfect walkers." That means they place their hind feet almost exactly in the prints made by their front feet.

11

NATE'S NOTES: How Cats Leap

One leap took Super Duper Hex from a sled on the ground to a tree branch high over Nate's head. Nate wanted to know: How could a monster cat do that?

1. Powerful back legs let cats jump as much as five times their own height.

2. Cats can twist into a good landing position. Their spines and tails have about 60 vertebrae, or round bones. Human spines have only about half that number.

3. Soft pads and sharp claws help cats land gently and hang on.

Residents of Buenos Aires, Argentina, tell the story of Minca—a cat who lived in a forty-foot tree for six years. They say she gave birth to three litters of kittens while up in the tree! Cat lovers passed her food on poles.

How to Make Ugly Cat Cupcakes

Cupcakes are tasty after a snowy day outside. These cupcakes look like Super Duper Hex. They're ugly.

Ask an adult to help you with this recipe. Makes 24 cupcakes.

GET TOGETHER:

- a muffin pan
- 24 paper or foil muffin cups
- 1 package of cake mix
- a mixing bowl
- a large spoon
- the oil, eggs, and water needed to make the cake (Look at the box for a list.)
- toothpicks
- a wire rack
- 18 pieces of string licorice (Black looks best, but you can use red if you don't like black.)

- scissors
- chocolate frosting (See the recipe starting on page 22, or use a can of prepared frosting.)
- 24 round cookies like Oreos, Nilla Wafers, or homemade sugar cookies
- 24 jelly beans, cut in half (Yellow and green look best.)
- 48 chocolate chips

MAKE YOUR CUPCAKES:

1. Preheat the oven according to the
   directions on the cake mix box.
2. Place the muffin cups in the pan.
3. Prepare the cake batter as directed on the
   box.
4. Spoon the batter into the cups, filling
   each one about $2/3$ full.

5. Bake 20 to 25 minutes, or until a toothpick inserted in the center of a cupcake comes out clean. Remove the cupcakes from the pan.

6. Cool the cupcakes on the wire rack for at least an hour. (You can get started on your cat face decorations while you wait.)

DECORATE YOUR CATS:

1. Using the scissors, cut 24 "cat tails" from the licorice. Each tail should be about as long as your middle finger.

2. Cut the rest of the licorice into "whiskers." The whiskers should be about half as long as the tails.

3. The cookies will be your cat faces. Use frosting as "glue" to attach licorice whiskers, jelly bean eyes, and chocolate chip ears. Let the faces dry for about 30 minutes.

4. Frost the cupcakes.
5. Stand one cat face on edge on top of each cupcake.
6. Place a tail on each cupcake behind the face.
7. Eat!

How to Make Chocolate Frosting

Frosting is the icing on a (cup)cake! It makes everything taste good.

Ask an adult to help you with this recipe. It will make enough frosting for 24 cupcakes or one cake.

GET TOGETHER:

- a saucepan
- a large spoon
- 2 cups of heavy cream
- a 16-ounce bag of semisweet chocolate chips
- 2 teaspoons of vanilla extract

MAKE YOUR FROSTING:

1. Heat the cream over low heat in the saucepan until it just bubbles.
2. Remove the saucepan from the heat.
3. Stir in the chocolate chips and the vanilla extract. Mix slowly until the chips are melted and the frosting is smooth.
4. Cool the frosting about 20 minutes so that it is easy to spread.

People Who Have Birthdays on July 12

Nate was born on July 12. He's not the only one. Here are some famous people who share Nate's birthday:

Julius Caesar—emperor of ancient Rome. Born in 100 BC.

Bill Cosby—a funny actor. Born in 1937.

Henry David Thoreau—a writer who lived in the woods around Walden Pond, Massachusetts. Born in 1817.

Kristi Yamaguchi—a gold medal–winning Olympic figure skater. Born in 1971.

Pablo Neruda—a great poet from Chile. Born in 1904.

Who Shares Your Birthday?

Try checking this book out of the library:
The Teacher's Calendar of Famous Birthdays
by Luisa Gerasimo.

Or look at this Web site:
www.kidsparties.com/birthdates.htm

Cat Jokes

Q: What's smarter than a talking cat?
A: A spelling bee!

Q: What do you call a cat who eats lemons?
A: A sourpuss!

Q: What's every cat's favorite song?
A: "Three Blind Mice"!

Q: What do cats eat for breakfast?
A: Mice Crispies!

Q: Did you hear the joke about the cat up a tree? Don't worry about it—it's over your head!

Have you helped solve all Nate the Great's mysteries?

❑ **Nate the Great**: Meet Nate, the great detective, and join him as he uses incredible sleuthing skills to solve his first big case.

❑ **Nate the Great Goes Undercover**: Who— or what—is raiding Oliver's trash every night? Nate bravely hides out in his friend's garbage can to catch the smelly crook.

❑ **Nate the Great and the Lost List**: Nate loves pancakes, but who ever heard of cats eating them? Is a strange recipe at the heart of this mystery?

❑ **Nate the Great and the Phony Clue**: Against ferocious cats, hostile adversaries, and a sly phony clue, Nate struggles to prove that he's still the greatest detective.

❑ **Nate the Great and the Sticky Case**: Nate is stuck with his stickiest case yet as he hunts for his friend Claude's valuable stegosaurus stamp.

❑ **Nate the Great and the Missing Key**: Nate isn't afraid to look anywhere—even under the nose of his friend's ferocious dog, Fang—to solve the case of the missing key.

❑ **Nate the Great and the Snowy Trail**: Nate has his work cut out for him when his friend Rosamond loses the birthday present she was going to give him. How can he find the present when Rosamond won't even tell him what it is?

❑ **Nate the Great and the Fishy Prize**: The trophy for the Smartest Pet Contest has disappeared! Will Sludge, Nate's clue-sniffing dog, help solve the case and prove he's worthy of the prize?

❑ **Nate the Great Stalks Stupidweed**: When his friend Oliver loses his special plant, Nate searches high and low. Who knew a little weed could be so tricky?

❑ **Nate the Great and the Boring Beach Bag**: It's no relaxing day at the beach for Nate and his trusty dog, Sludge, as they search through sand and surf for signs of a missing beach bag.

❑ **Nate the Great Goes Down in the Dumps**: Nate discovers that the only way to clean up this case is to visit the town dump. Detective work can sure get dirty!

❑ **Nate the Great and the Halloween Hunt**: It's Halloween, but Nate isn't trick-or-treating for candy. Can any of the witches, pirates, and robots he meets help him find a missing cat?

❑ **Nate the Great and the Musical Note**: Nate is used to looking for clues, not listening for them! When he gets caught in the middle of a musical riddle, can he hear his way out?

❏ **Nate the Great and the Stolen Base**: It's not easy to track down a stolen base, and Nate's hunt leads him to some strange places before he finds himself at bat once more.

❏ **Nate the Great and the Pillowcase**: When a pillowcase goes missing, Nate must venture into the dead of night to search for clues. Everyone sleeps easier knowing Nate the Great is on the case!

❏ **Nate the Great and the Mushy Valentine**: Nate hates mushy stuff. But when someone leaves a big heart taped to Sludge's doghouse, Nate must help his favorite pooch discover his secret admirer.

❏ **Nate the Great and the Tardy Tortoise**: Where did the mysterious green tortoise in Nate's yard come from? Nate needs all his patience to follow this slow . . . slow . . . clue.

❏ **Nate the Great and the Crunchy Christmas**: It's Christmas, and Fang, Annie's scary dog, is not feeling jolly. Can Nate find Fang's crunchy Christmas mail before Fang crunches on *him*?

❏ **Nate the Great Saves the King of Sweden**: Can Nate solve his *first-ever* international case without leaving his own neighborhood?

❏ **Nate the Great and Me: The Case of the Fleeing Fang**: A surprise Happy Detective Day party is great fun for Nate until his friend's dog disappears! Help Nate track down the missing pooch, and learn all the tricks of the trade in a special fun section for aspiring detectives.

❑ **Nate the Great and the Monster Mess**: Nate loves his mother's deliciously spooky Monster Cookies, but the recipe has vanished! This is one case Nate and his growling stomach can't afford to lose.

❑ **Nate the Great, San Francisco Detective**: Nate visits his cousin Olivia Sharp in the big city, but it's no vacation. Can he find a lost joke book in time to save the world?

❑ **Nate the Great and the Big Sniff**: Nate depends on his dog, Sludge, to help him solve all his cases. But Nate is on his own this time, because Sludge has disappeared! Can Nate solve the case and recover his canine buddy?

❑ **Nate the Great on the Owl Express**: Nate boards a train to guard Hoot, his cousin Olivia Sharp's pet owl. Then Hoot vanishes! Can Nate find out *whooo* took the feathered creature?